MW00897875

ARK TALES

WILLIAM E HOUGH

ILLUSTRATED BY NATASSIA SCORESBY

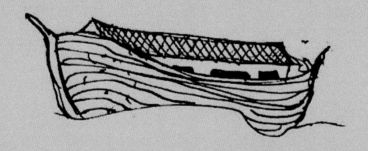

Text Copyright © 2010 by Jenn Hough /Illustrations copyright © 2019 Natassia Scoresby

All rights reserved. This book or any portion thereof may not be reproduced or used in any manner whatsoever without the express written permission of the publisherexcept for the use of brief quotations in a book review.

Printed in the United States of America

First Printing, 2019

ISBN 9781688763890

Independently published

In October 2010, my father-in-law, William E. Hough (affectionately known as "Doc" to most of us) emailed me a file that he wanted me to look over. He had an idea for a children's book and wanted my feedback as an elementary school teacher. After hearing H. David Burton's talk "Let Virtue Garnish Your Thoughts" during the Latter-day Saint general conference in October 2009, Doc felt prompted to do something to help bring these virtues to light. An excerpt from that talk explains: "We need not be a part of the virtue malaise that is penetrating and infecting society. If we follow the world in abandoning Christian-centered virtues, the consequences may be disastrous...We need to stand tall and be firmly fixed in perpetuating Christlike virtues, even the "ity" virtues [charity, humility, etc.], in our everyday lives. Teaching virtuous traits begins in the home with parents who care and set the example." Similar to fables, Doc wanted to create a tool that could help teach these twelve important virtues to young children using familiar, non-human characters in a world that is quickly losing its fundamental values.

Doc and his wife were planning a visit to see my family just a couple weeks after he sent me the file called "Ark Tales" and suggested we could sit down together and discuss it more in person. Well, once they arrived at our home, Doc was so busy being a great grandpa and dad that we never did get around to talking about how to make those stories into a book.

Weeks turned into months. Months turned into years. Doc passed away rather unexpectedly on August 13, 2017. Eighteen months later, I stumbled across the file "Ark Tales" on my hard drive. I just sat there, staring at the document I hadn't seen in almost ten years, deeply saddened that Doc and I never worked on this while we had the chance to try and bring his little book of virtues to fruition. But it didn't take long before I was filled with a small glimmer of hope. I suddenly thought of my friend, Natassia, who is an incredibly gifted graphic artist and illustrator. I asked Natassia if I could commission her to bring these stories to life, just as they were, to help me share Doc's legacy as a gift for his family and future posterity. And Ark Tales became a reality.

I'd like to first dedicate this book, posthumously, in loving memory to our one-of-a-kind Doc. Beloved husband, dad, father-in-law, grandpa, brother, physician, colleague, spiritual leader, friend, neighbor, hunter, fisherman, gardener, and a die hard Dallas Cowboys and St. Louis Cardinals fan.

And to all those whose lives Doc touched and will continue to touch with Ark Tales, but most especially:

His wife--Karole

His children--Kevin, Jared, and Nicole

and His 16 grandchildren--James, Emma, Cole, Connor, Garrett, Olivia, Ayzlynn and Korbin, Jacob, Cooper, Karcyn, Calvin and JJ, Daniel, HaileyJane and Karyana.

-Jenn Hough, April 2019

For Aislinn, Nathan, Wesley, Benji, & Owen -NS

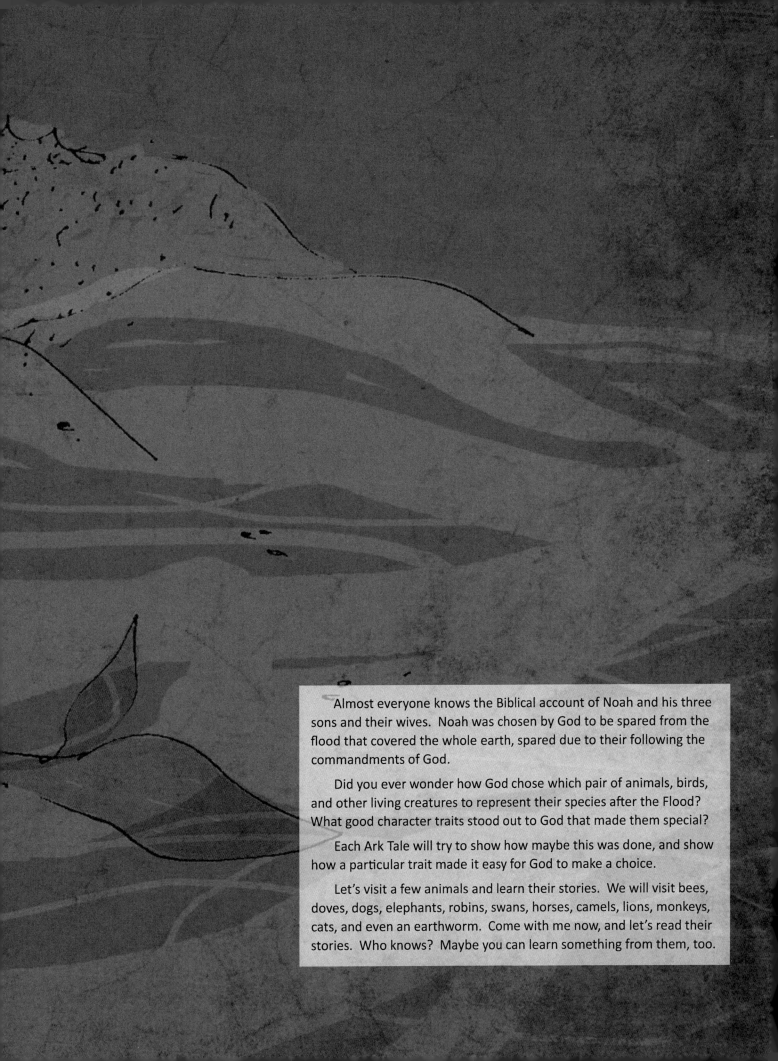

Almost everyone knows the Biblical account of Noah and his three sons and their wives. Noah was chosen by God to be spared from the flood that covered the whole earth, spared due to their following the commandments of God.

Did you ever wonder how God chose which pair of animals, birds, and other living creatures to represent their species after the Flood? What good character traits stood out to God that made them special?

Each Ark Tale will try to show how maybe this was done, and show how a particular trait made it easy for God to make a choice.

Let's visit a few animals and learn their stories. We will visit bees, doves, dogs, elephants, robins, swans, horses, camels, lions, monkeys, cats, and even an earthworm. Come with me now, and let's read their stories. Who knows? Maybe you can learn something from them, too.

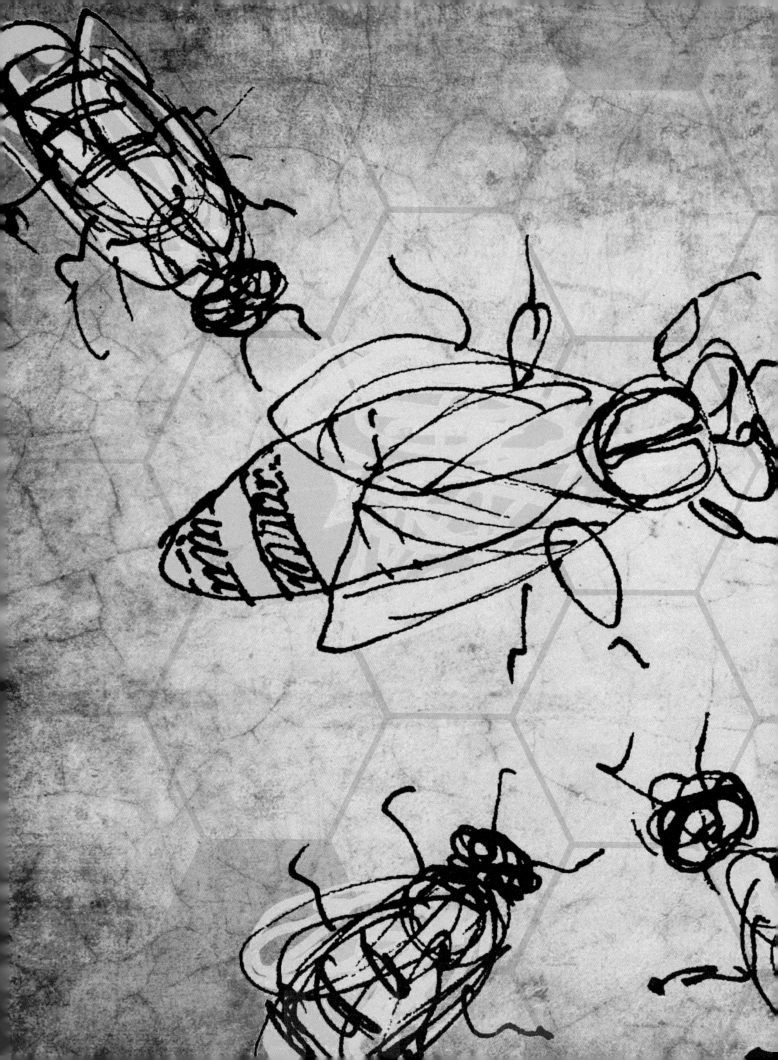

GENEROSITY

Queen Bee sat in her throne room, surrounded by her worker bees, and thought of what she had just been told by some of her most trusted friends.

Some of the other beehives had decided to pollinate only some flowers and not others. They had even decided to withhold their production of honey to only certain people.

So Queen Bee thought she would go and visit other hives. She would find out what was happening among the flowers, the fruits, the vegetables, and all her friends in the plant world that she had known all her life.

When Queen Bee went to visit her brother and sister hives, she became very disturbed by what she found out. One beehive decided to pollinate only red flowers. Another beehive said they would do only yellow ones. Another refused to pollinate any fruit trees, and still another hive said they would not fly to any of the vegetables. They all said they would not share their honey if anyone was too short or too fat or if they came from a different country. What had happened to their generosity?

Queen Bee remembered that this was not what she and her hive had been taught. They had been taught by their queen, and all the queens all the way back to the Garden of Eden, what their special duty was. They had been charged by their Creator to bless all the plants and flowers, and to provide honey to everyone for sweetness in their cooking and to put on their bread.

When Queen Bee returned to her hive, she was sad. She was not very proud of her brother and sister beehives.

However, that night, when Queen Bee was at rest, she received a message from the Creator. She and her hive had been chosen to represent her species as the world was about to be cleansed. She was to know who God's prophet was, and when this would happen.

The time came on a cloudy rainy day when a man named Noah came and collected her hive. Queen Bee and her hive blessed Noah and his family during the Flood, and honey bees have been blessing people by their generosity all over the world ever since.

RESPONSIBILITY

Billy Mourning Dove awoke suddenly from his sleep. He remembered that it was his turn today to go looking for water and food for the flock. However, just as he was about to leave, he was stopped by several of his friends who said they would be skipping their jobs today. They wanted to do some stunts and trick flying, and they were going to make this a play day.

Billy thought this was wrong. He decided to go talk to his best friend and secret girlfriend, Suzy, about this.

Suzy was on her way to find Billy when they met each other. They settled together on the branch of an olive tree. She was upset about the same thing as Billy was. She said the other lady doves had gone to have fun instead of gathering sticks and straw.

"We need the sticks and straw for building nests for the upcoming season. We'll all be choosing mates soon," Suzy said.

"And without food and water," Billy added, "we cannot survive."

Suzy nodded. "Without the nests, how are we to be ready to take care of our new little ones?" she asked.

Both Suzy and Billy knew it was their responsibility to take good care of them -selves, and to prepare for their future families. While the other doves were out playing, Suzy and Billy worked on their jobs all that day,

and returned to the flock knowing they had done their best.

When they went to sleep that night, they tucked their heads under their wings, as birds do when they are sleeping. But it was a restless sleep, because they were worried about their foolish friends.

During the night, they were visited by the Comforter. He had visited them before when they were troubled. This time the Comforter brought a message from the Creator of an upcoming event that was very important. Both Billy and Suzy had been chosen for a very special calling. God's prophet would let them know when it was time for them to come join him.

On a rainy stormy day Suzy and Billy flew together where they joined the family of Noah, God's prophet. Noah took Suzy aside and said, "When our journey is ended, you will be given a very special task."

Suzy and Billy were chosen to go on the Ark because Noah knew that they would be obedient. They had proved that they could be given important tasks and they would carry out their responsibilities.

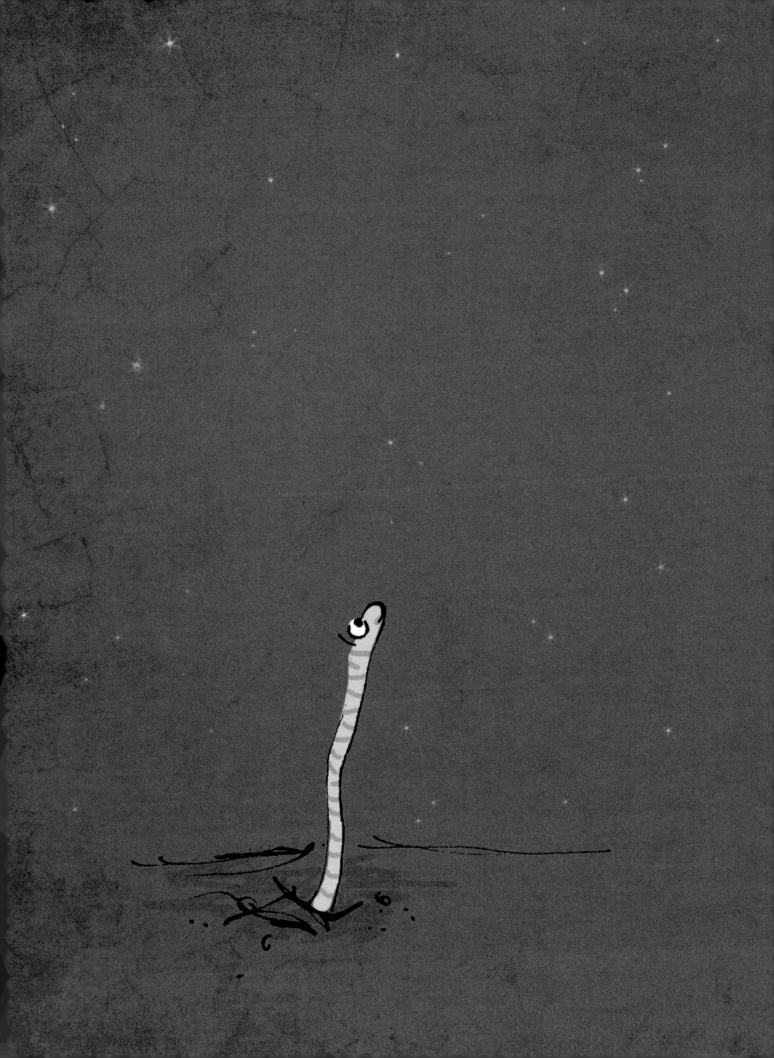

HUMILITY

IB Long was an earthworm, but not just any kind of worm. He was actually a night crawler. He was a night being because the bright light of day made him sick.

IB lived in a place where the above-ground creatures would never go, but for him it was perfect. He shared with his fellow night crawlers places like swamps, gardens, compost heaps, and garbage dumps. This to him was paradise.

For this reason, he and his fellow worms were looked down on and thought to be useless.

Even worms have feelings. One day when he was feeling sad, he was suddenly brought to the surface and was face-to-face with a human.

Now IB had known something about humans, but never like this. Strangely this human had the ability to talk to IB, and even stranger was that IB could understand him.

"My name is Noah," the human said. "Do I have the pleasure of addressing IB Long, the night crawler?"

"Yes," said IB excitedly. "That is my name!"

"I have need of your services, and need many of your fellow earthworms as well," said Noah.

IB was curious. "How could we possibly be of service to you?"

Noah smiled at him. "In your humble life, you do far more good than you realize. You take that which was thrown away and turn it back to good. You take soil which will not grow anything well, and turn it into good soil. You do all this while being scorned by your fellow creatures."

"I didn't realize I could do that," said IB.

Noah nodded. "Oh, yes. For this reason, the Creator wants you and your friends to be with us on the Ark. You will be very important to help restore the earth after the Flood."

IB Long felt like he was suddenly more than just a "lowly" worm. He went on the Ark with Noah and his family. He did fulfill his destiny to replenish the soil after the Flood.

In fact, one of his future descendents would include a famous worm who starred in many children's books written by Richard Scarry.

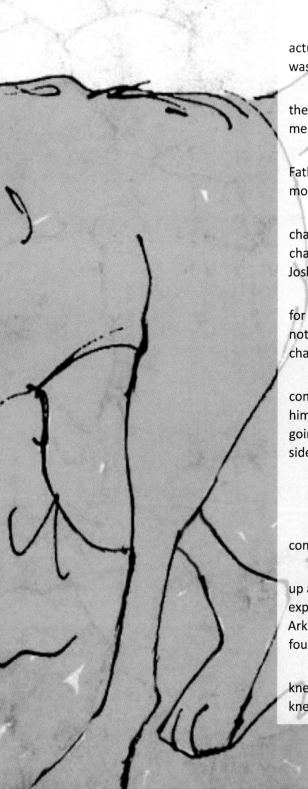

FIDELITY

Joshua was just a plain, ordinary dog. He was not a purebred, but actually a little bit of every breed that was known at the time of Noah. He wasn't big. He wasn't handsome. He was just plain.

What was it that caught the attention of Shem, son of Noah? Joshua the dog was a perfect example of what fidelity was all about. Fidelity means faithful, and Joshua was certainly that.

When Shem's wife was going to the market to gather food by order of Father Noah, she was attacked by people who wanted to take away her money. Joshua was there to protect her and drive away the bad people.

Father Noah tried to warn the people of what they needed to do to change their ways, and warned of what was going to happen if they didn't change. This made people mad, and they would throw rocks at Noah. Joshua was there to protect him.

For this reason, his devotion and loyalty, Joshua was a perfect choice for what Father Noah knew was coming. The problem was, Joshua did not have a mate. It wasn't long, however, before something happened to change all that.

Father Noah was going about one day, warning the people as he was commanded to, but the crowd was very angry. Joshua tried to protect him, but there were too many angry people. Just when everything was going bad, suddenly there was help from another dog. She stood side by side with Joshua, and soon the mob was scared away.

Who was this helper?

"My name is Natalie," said Joshua's new friend.

Joshua was curious. A female dog, a good and faithful servant, had come to help him. He had never known that before.

"Thank you, Natalie, for your help," said Father Noah. Joshua looked up at his master. "She is the faithful companion of my son Ham's family," explained Father Noah. "She is to be your companion and mate on my Ark. You both carry the good qualities of your species. You will be the foundation for future generations."

Joshua and Natalie looked at each other with doggy smiles. They knew what how important it was to be faithful to their families. They knew Father Noah was right.

ACCOUNTABILITY

Carl the Camel stood strong next to his mate Carla. They were in the corral beside the tents of Ahab. Ahab was talking to a man who was familiar to both Carl and Carla.

Ahab was a camel broker and a caravan merchant. He was talking to Noah the prophet, who was thought by most to be crazy. Noah was always talking about what was coming and for the need to repent. Ahab said times were good to make money and have fun.

"Which pair of your camels is the most reliable? Which can you depend on no matter what the hardships are?" asked Noah.

Now Ahab knew it was Carl and Carla, but he wanted to get rid of a pair that were lazy and not always accountable. He pointed to two other camels.

"These two right here," said Ahab. "I'll give you a good deal, the both of them for just 200 shekels."

Now, Noah knew when he got to the camel broker's tents that Carl and Carla were the pair that he needed. The still small voice of the Holy Spirit had told him so.

Carl and Carla also knew that the man Noah would be coming for them that day. The still small voice had told them what was to happen.

Noah shook his head. "No," he said. He pointed to Carl and Carla. "I want that pair, and you will give them to me for nothing."

Ahab said, "I will what? Of course not!"

Noah just smiled at him. "Yes, you will, just as you were instructed in your dream."

Ahab was astonished. "You know about that?"

"Yes," Noah replied, "I know that and much more, which would cause you problems in the future."

Ahab rushed into the corral and gathered up the lead ropes. "Here, take them and go quickly!"

The stories of how Carl and Carla were able to carry heavy loads across large deserts without water were known to everyone. They never failed to do their job. When they were young, they had been taught by their mothers and fathers to do their best now and even better later. They were also taught that if they didn't do their best, to admit it and do better next time. They were taught in all things to be accountable.

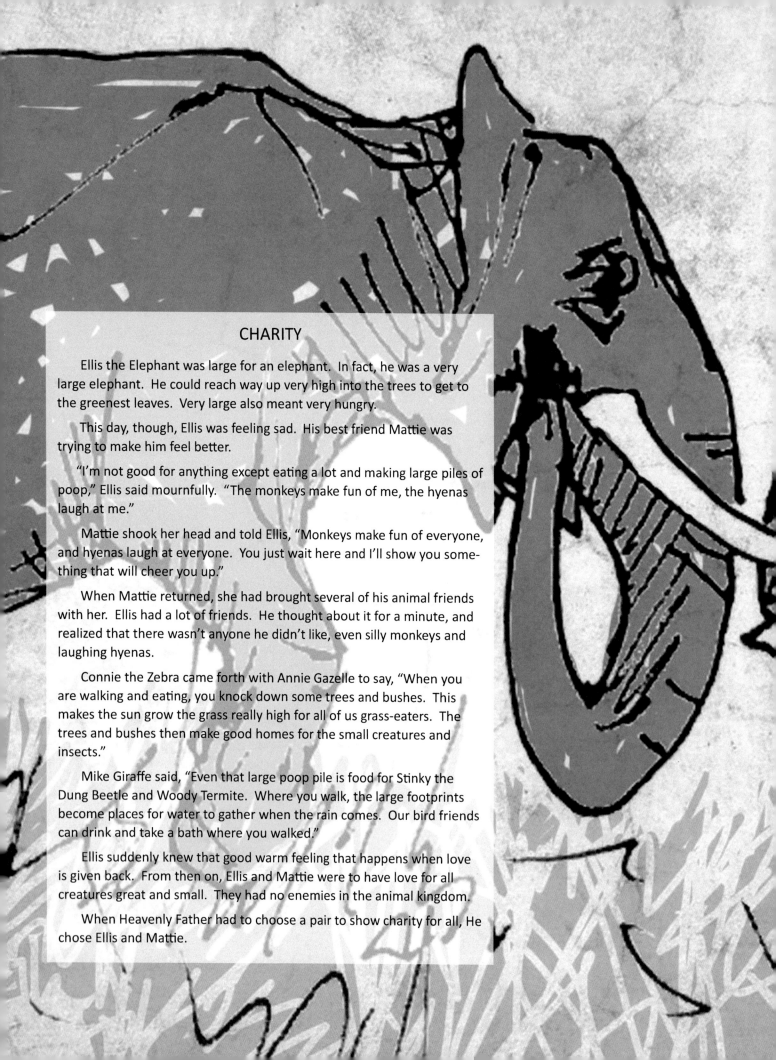

CHARITY

Ellis the Elephant was large for an elephant. In fact, he was a very large elephant. He could reach way up very high into the trees to get to the greenest leaves. Very large also meant very hungry.

This day, though, Ellis was feeling sad. His best friend Mattie was trying to make him feel better.

"I'm not good for anything except eating a lot and making large piles of poop," Ellis said mournfully. "The monkeys make fun of me, the hyenas laugh at me."

Mattie shook her head and told Ellis, "Monkeys make fun of everyone, and hyenas laugh at everyone. You just wait here and I'll show you something that will cheer you up."

When Mattie returned, she had brought several of his animal friends with her. Ellis had a lot of friends. He thought about it for a minute, and realized that there wasn't anyone he didn't like, even silly monkeys and laughing hyenas.

Connie the Zebra came forth with Annie Gazelle to say, "When you are walking and eating, you knock down some trees and bushes. This makes the sun grow the grass really high for all of us grass-eaters. The trees and bushes then make good homes for the small creatures and insects."

Mike Giraffe said, "Even that large poop pile is food for Stinky the Dung Beetle and Woody Termite. Where you walk, the large footprints become places for water to gather when the rain comes. Our bird friends can drink and take a bath where you walked."

Ellis suddenly knew that good warm feeling that happens when love is given back. From then on, Ellis and Mattie were to have love for all creatures great and small. They had no enemies in the animal kingdom.

When Heavenly Father had to choose a pair to show charity for all, He chose Ellis and Mattie.

SPIRITUALITY

"Some things are just always correct. They are sacred," said Tom, the long-haired yellow cat.

"Like what?" asked Spike, his younger brother. "I think nothing is sacred. I can say or do anything I want!" He arched his back and ruffled his fur. "I have the right to choose."

Tom looked at him very seriously. "The right to choose, yes. But with choice comes consequences. Choose right: Good consequences. Choose wrong: Bad consequences."

Joining in on the discussion was Jill, the very pretty long-haired neighbor cat.

"Using our Heavenly Father's name in the right way is sacred," she said to Spike.

"Being quiet and reverent in church is sacred.

"Showing respect to your mother and father is sacred.

"Always telling the truth is sacred."

Tom agreed with Jill. "I know when I obey these commandments, I get good goose bumps and I feel warm inside."

"Me, too!" said Jill.

Tom and Jill knew that spirituality is holding sacred all things spiritual. It was a quality that Noah knew must go with him and his family on the Ark. It would be a very important quality in the world following the Flood.

Tom and Jill were purr-fect examples of spirituality, and they were chosen to join Noah and his family on the Ark.

MORALITY

Penny was a pen, that is, a female swan. Her life mate was Chuck, a cob, a male swan. They were mated for life. They had been together for as long as they had memory. So had their fathers and mothers before them for as long as they remembered.

Both Penny and Chuck had been taught by their parents that certain things were always correct in their behavior toward others, and that in these things, there were no exceptions.

Life mates are forever.

Friends are to be cherished.

Help those in need without expecting praise.

These are some of the standards that were part of the moral code of conduct. Because Penny and Chuck lived by these standards, it made Noah's choice to have them join his family and the other animals on the Ark an easy one.

Penny and Chuck did go on the Ark, and to this day, all swans mate for life.

CHASTITY

Roy Robin greeted the bright sunny day as always with awake-up whistle which was immediately answered by Mother and Father Robin.

Roy had never known anything in his family but Mother and Father Robin, but he was now ready to leave the nest and go out on his own. It was time for Father to take Roy aside to talk to his son.

"Do you ever notice a difference in us and the other bird families?" asked Father Robin.

Roy thought a minute. "No, not really," he replied.

Father asked, "Have you ever known any other family except us and your older brothers and sisters?"

"No," said Roy. "It has always been just you, Mother Robin, and my brothers and sisters.

Father nodded. "All right. Now think about your other bird friends and tell me what is different in their families."

"Well," said Roy, "none that I know have the same mother and father in their nests. It's kind of mixed up, because the mothers and fathers don't stay together."

"That's right," said Father. You see, our species choose their mates for always. We are among the few bird species who are together forever. This binds us closer together as a family. As you leave our nest, Mother Robin and I want you to know that this is how the Creator wants it to be also with you."

So when Roy left the family nest, it was not very long before he met his chosen mate for life. Her name was Carol, and the circle of life and family continued.

It was an easy decision for Noah to choose Roy and Carol to be part of the Ark family. Knowing that being true and faithful in marriage, which is the virtue of chastity, was something worth keeping.

CIVILITY

Monkeys being civil is usually not something that goes together. They are loud, curious (like George), and usually not nice. They like to be in places they should not be, do things they should not do, and say things they should not say.

This is why Annie was not your typical monkey. She was polite, quiet, and courteous of others' feelings. No, she was not a typical monkey.

One day her friends were being very bad to Ellis the Elephant – calling him fat and stupid, laughing at him and making him sad. Annie tried to get them to stop, but they just started on her, too, calling her unkind names.

Just when Annie was about to break down and cry, she saw a familiar kind face among the other monkeys. It was her secret boyfriend, Jeremy, the leader of another band of monkeys. He stepped in to put an end to the bullying. But the others would not stop.

"I'm sorry," said Jeremy. "I'm afraid this behavior has gotten out of hand. Even I can't control it. I think you are the only monkey who has any good behavior."

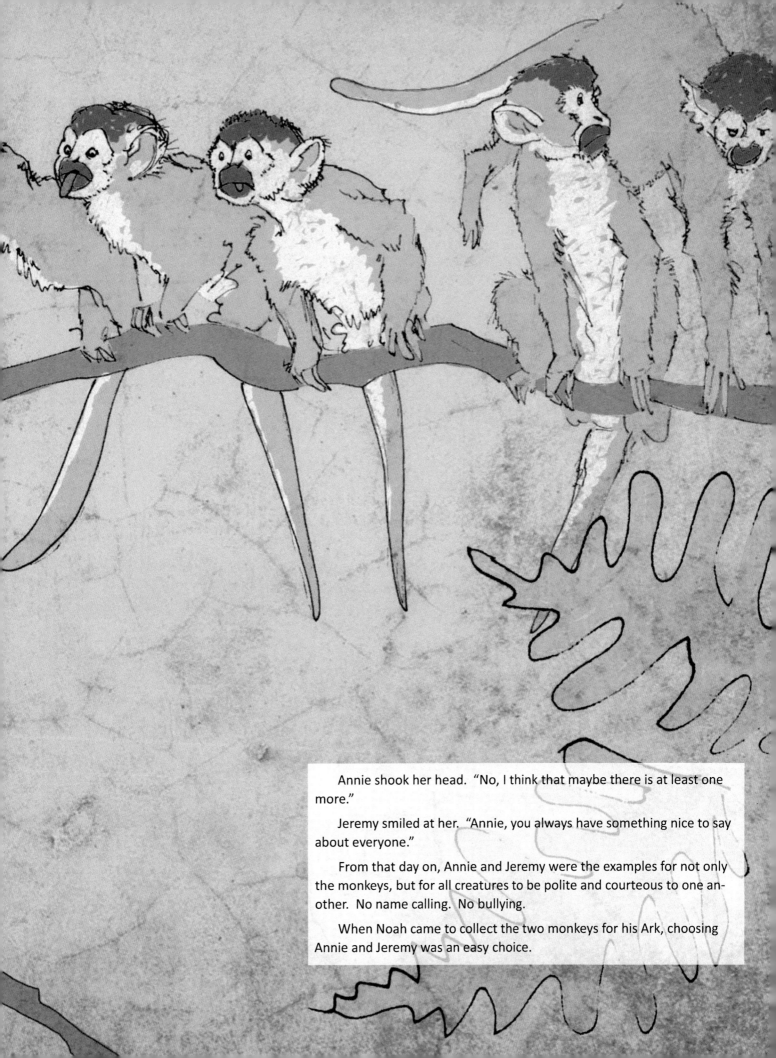

Annie shook her head. "No, I think that maybe there is at least one more."

Jeremy smiled at her. "Annie, you always have something nice to say about everyone."

From that day on, Annie and Jeremy were the examples for not only the monkeys, but for all creatures to be polite and courteous to one another. No name calling. No bullying.

When Noah came to collect the two monkeys for his Ark, choosing Annie and Jeremy was an easy choice.

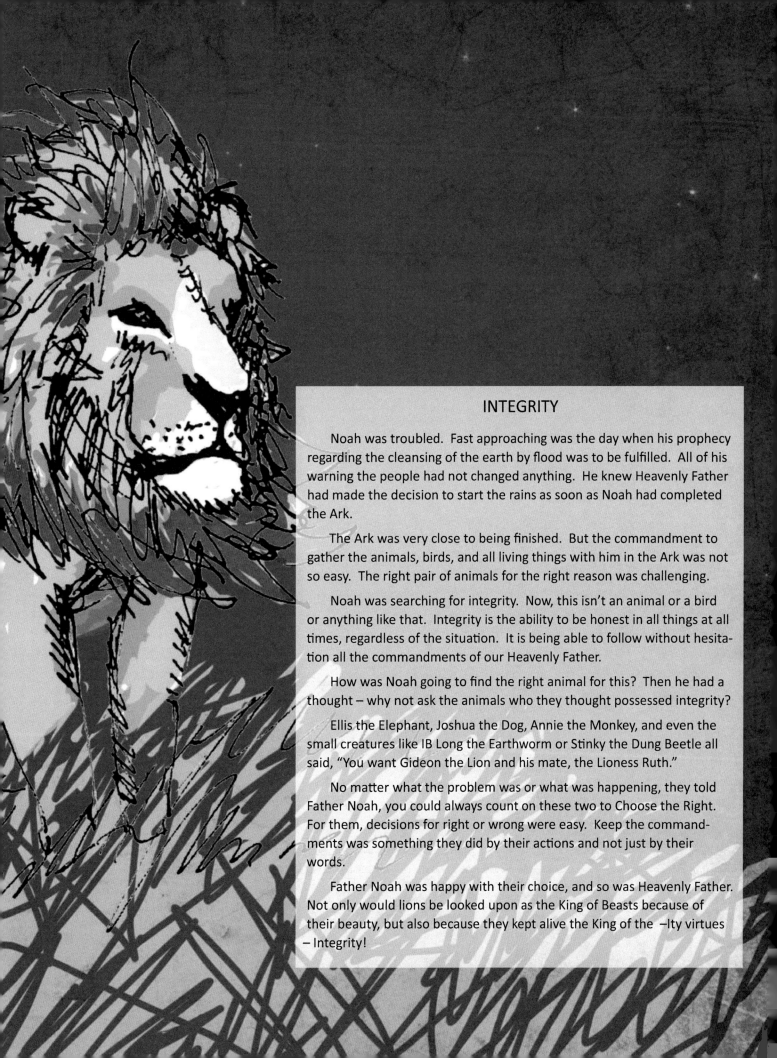

INTEGRITY

Noah was troubled. Fast approaching was the day when his prophecy regarding the cleansing of the earth by flood was to be fulfilled. All of his warning the people had not changed anything. He knew Heavenly Father had made the decision to start the rains as soon as Noah had completed the Ark.

The Ark was very close to being finished. But the commandment to gather the animals, birds, and all living things with him in the Ark was not so easy. The right pair of animals for the right reason was challenging.

Noah was searching for integrity. Now, this isn't an animal or a bird or anything like that. Integrity is the ability to be honest in all things at all times, regardless of the situation. It is being able to follow without hesitation all the commandments of our Heavenly Father.

How was Noah going to find the right animal for this? Then he had a thought – why not ask the animals who they thought possessed integrity?

Ellis the Elephant, Joshua the Dog, Annie the Monkey, and even the small creatures like IB Long the Earthworm or Stinky the Dung Beetle all said, "You want Gideon the Lion and his mate, the Lioness Ruth."

No matter what the problem was or what was happening, they told Father Noah, you could always count on these two to Choose the Right. For them, decisions for right or wrong were easy. Keep the commandments was something they did by their actions and not just by their words.

Father Noah was happy with their choice, and so was Heavenly Father. Not only would lions be looked upon as the King of Beasts because of their beauty, but also because they kept alive the King of the –Ity virtues – Integrity!

DIGNITY

It was a time of great confusion for both mankind and also for the animal world. Among the animals, none was more confused than Henry the dapple gray stallion.

As horses go, Henry was handsome, but not like Prince, the sheik's black Arabian horse. Prince had the best saddle, jewels on his bridle, rings in his ears, and even a "Hot Stuff" tattoo on his hind quarters.

Henry wondered if he should be more like Prince.

"No, Henry, that is just not you," said Abigail, Henry's cute filly friend. "Al the young colts and fillies are choosing to also pierce their bodies and have tattoos, but remember what we have been told by Noah the Prophet."

"I know," replied Henry. "But to be cool, you have to be like Prince."

Abigail shook her head. "Do you remember what Noah said to us last week?"

Henry snorted. "Yes, but you know most people say Noah is crazy."

Abigail asked him, very quietly, "And what do you think?"

Henry hung his head. He knew he was only repeating gossip. He also knew the answer would come only with prayer. He trotted away from Abigail and found a place where he could pray and ask Heavenly Father for some answers.

He found out, as he prayed, answers he actually knew before he started. He knew he wasn't Prince. He was simply Henry. And Henry did not need tattoos, earrings, fancy bridles and saddles. He only needed to be himself.

He also was told that he and Abigail would be chosen by Noah to go with the family on the Ark. It was not because he was a fancy horse. It was because by being themselves, he and Abigail had dignity, a quality worth saving forever.